Harald Neugebauer – The Editor

nF235617

Harald Neugebauer

THE EDITOR

Derya Yalimcan e.K.
Hauptstraße 62,
De-07937 Langenwolschendorf

© 2021 (German), 2022 (English) Harald Neugebauer
Language editing: GittaWolf

Production and publishing:
BoD - Books on Demand, Norderstedt

ISBN 978-3-7568-0002-5

As long as you play chess, you depend on moves directed at your opponent. This changes when you start thinking about the game itself rather than the movements.

Ernst Jünger's Commentary on Friedrich Georg's 70th Birthday

Prologue

Her curly, henna-red hair sparkled in the evening sun that shone in through the window. The young-at-heart woman in her mid-fifties, who could be mistaken for someone in her late twenties by her style of dress, was one of the last representatives of the truly free and independent press in Western Europe. She looked out of the window onto the Danube, paused for a moment and continued to whisper into her dictaphone:

"Today, Europe is no longer free. The culmination will hopefully result in a great, united resistance. We are organizing against all expectations in Eastern Poland ... Poland seems to be the only state besides Hungary that has not yet been infiltrated. We do not have many allies ... But before that, I will describe, for the sake of posterity, from the very beginning the story of which the Austrian book editor Dr. Harald Neugebauer tragically became an eyewitness and one of the protagonists. He told me his story before the Battle of Brussels-Molenbeek, and substantiated it with the diary entries, writings and notes that I use as the basis for this manuscript."

Kimberly M., Budapest, Hungary, Free Europe

Berlin-Zehlendorf, Dr. Neugebauer

The editor reopened the first page of the book and began to read again:

Early autumn in Graubünden. The wind blowing cold announced the impending arrival of a frosty winter.

The dense fir forest on the mountainside was swaying back and forth in the autumnal wind, a many-voiced chorus heralding the approaching cold season.

A man, sitting on the shore of the lake, took off his oval-shaped silver-plated reading glasses and looked out over Lake Silvaplana. He breathed deeply, filling his lungs with the damp, cold, clear air, and continued to watch the snow-covered mountain peaks, where the sharp light of the September sun refracted as if in a prism. He felt a little shivery, so he slammed shut the book he was holding and stood up from the park bench at the edge of the lake. "Am I Prometheus or Epimetheus?" he asked himself as he walked back home, following the shore. It was time to leave Sils and go to Basel. As he noticed out of the corner of his eye the cold waters of Lake Silvaplana to his left, he realized that the deep dark water attracted him in a deeply emotional way. "I want to sink down in you," he whispered and stopped. "If the water came up to me, I wouldn't refuse it," he muttered softly to himself. Turning slowly to the left, he walked leisurely toward the water. The water, dark and calm, spoke to him: "Into me you can sink forever. For I am faithful to thee, not am I man that I can refuse thee faithfulness. Come, come, O sink into me, as every tear drop that will fill me." The man approached the water without haste, in small steps. His brown suede shoes touched the wet and he was overcome for a brief moment by the coldness of the water soaking his feet. "Waterdrop I want to become and be submerged within you." He held his breath until his lungs began to burn, wondering how long it would be before he drowned in the cold water.

"But are you ready for me, O you fire of Prometheus? Thou eternal knowledge? Not that thou shouldst dry on my flame," the man said, adding: "Some other time perhaps, but not today." "Down the mountain I will go to tell men what there is to say," he declared in a determined and stern voice. His mind was on the edge of a precipice lost in the deep immensity of the lake. "Not yet," he spoke to himself. "Not yet; first I must articulate it."

"To hold up the mirror to men, to make clear to them their vulgar banality, and to educate man and beast with the sledgehammer," he whispered to the lake. "I have overcome even you, Arthur," he said, "my mentor, who now is nothing but the eristic demagogue, nothing more ..." The words "The barren polar bear zones" slipped out of his mouth as his gaze was lost among the snow-covered mountain peaks. "Failed at teaching," he spoke, looking out toward the lake again, deep in thought. "The loss of man and God."

"So long, eternal friend, I know you will wait for me patiently until we meet again ..." Wordlessly, he continued to watch the lake until a delicate female hand touched his right shoulder from behind. The woman in the long black dress let her left hand rest on him. She looked down at him with glazed and sorrowful eyes: "Your shoes are wet, come home. You need to dry your feet, or you'll catch a cold."

As they walked home, the woman on his right tucked her arm into his. "You must forget her," she said. "Learn to forget her. Write. Writing is good for you. I'll help you pack your things." "Will you stop talking to me about her! You banal soul, you can't understand," he replied angrily. She looked at him and remained silent. The man thought for a moment, then said: "I want to go to Rapallo, by myself. I'm not going with you, sister. Tell mother that all is well." "No," she said, shocked. "Nothing is well."

"You are utterly depressed, and more isolation will make you even more ill. Please come with me." "No sister, finish packing my things, I'm going to Italy. In Rapallo I will be able to write in peace. And I'm going alone, most certainly!" he murmured, growing louder. "To Bertha I will write another letter." "Who is Bertha?" his sister asked in amazement. "The lady of my delight," he said. "You want to go to Rapallo without saying goodbye in person? Why must you always push people away?" she asked angrily. "You can't keep rebuking everyone with your radical ways!"

*

Sitting in the first-class carriage, the man saw through the window how his sister, sad-faced and with tears in her eyes, waved a sorrow goodbye to him with her right hand. He waved back at her stiffly, and as the train pulled away, he took the daily paper, Basler Nachrichten, out of his jacket pocket and looked at the front page. "Failed assassination attempt on Wilhelm Friedrich Ludwig of Prussia and the assembled princes," it said. He read on with moderate interest. Anarchists were planning to assassinate William the First with dynamite! "Anarchists are would-be nihilists," he muttered, "would-be but unable-to-be nihilists." The cover story interested him only rudimentarily. So he turned the page and skimmed the next few pages. The report on the new law initiated by Bismarck to introduce health insurance in the German Empire, which was controversial but highly praised, gave him pause for a moment. "You claim your rights, they are not handed to you," he thought. In the back pages, he read about the aftermath of the Tiszaeszlár affair, which was still ongoing. A peasant girl had disappeared, and the girl's mother had filed charges against Jews. These were charged with alleged ritual murder for the Passover festival but were acquitted. Mass unrest had broken out in northeastern Hungary. The Danube monarchy was seething. "Richard," he said, "my faithful friend, as once you were. You are the pepper and salt of this decadence. Thee will I educate in writing, that thou mayest learn the superhuman, thou who art the sun of the downfall." He slammed the paper shut again, folded it carefully, and asked himself in his mind: "How shall mankind help itself, in spite of mankind?" Ivan Turgenev had died barely a month ago. "The realist," he exclaimed, in a low voice. He thought of the protagonist, Chulkaturin, in Turgenev's 'Diary of a Superfluous Man'. "Mankind," he said, looking through the compartment window into the ravine they were passing. "How far down could a man fall in such a ravine," he wondered. "Tell me, Chulkaturin!" He looked down into the gorge and tried to estimate the depth. "Man is a rope, suspended between beast and superman, he is a downfall and a transition," he thought. "But you are not deep enough for me to fall within you, for I am deeper than you," he said. He closed his eyes and fell into a shallow and restless sleep.

The editor looked up from the text. The final correction of the first part was now complete. But he didn't like the portrayal of Rapallo at all, and he decided to redo the entire description of the small Italian town, jotting the following note in his script:

DESCRIPTION RAPALLO

By now, he knew the text almost by heart. Normally, he wrote bachelor's and master's theses as a ghostwriter. After graduating in anthropology, he had preferred to continue his studies instead of working as an anthropologist. Society as a whole was sick, not sick with any viruses, but mentally sick, he was sure of it. What would happen, he wondered, if suddenly there were no more psychotropic drugs, and he laughed to himself. Now he was correcting the book of some intellectual bourgeois who had written his debut novella as the conclusion of his study of literature. The author tried to set a monument to his intellectual snobbery by writing a book that most likely no one would ever read except a select few from circles interested in literature, because the subject matter of this novella was simply too abstract. But since the payment was good, Dr. Neugebauer had accepted this assignment. Fortunately, the work was soon finished, and the text edited throughout, except for the pointless and boring description of the small Italian town of Rapallo.

Dr. Neugebauer continued reading the text:

Sitting at an old escritoire, he had been writing excessively, as if driven, for the past ten days, interrupted only by some short breaks for sleep and food. Overtired but relatively balanced, he wrote down the last line in the manuscript:

"End of part one"

The man closed the manuscript, leaned his back against the chair's backrest and stretched, reaching his arms up in the air, hands clasped. Briefly, he looked out the window in the direction of the castle and further out to sea ... The oil lamp had been burning continuously for ten days. The man extinguished the meager flame and thought: "This is about all the people, but no one will feel addressed ..." Then he took a blank sheet of paper on which he would write the title, glanced longingly in the direction of the bed, and loudly said to himself: "Sleep is death's little friend." And he wrote:

Thus Spoke Zarathustra.
A book for all and none
by
Friedrich Nietzsche

The editor looked up from the text again and wondered why anyone should be interested in German history, starting with Nietzsche. After studying literature for a long time, Paskowiak, the client, had only just managed to create average German literature. To give the book a little more substance, the editor added his own chapters that had not originally been included. He looked at the chapters he had, on a whim, added himself, just because he enjoyed it. But the real reason was simply that he was able to, and that he was a far better man of letters than Zoltan Paskowiak. Dr. Neugebauer's profession was cultural anthropology. But he was not to be underestimated as an amateur literary man either. Thus the 'epochal work' of the 'wanna be' Magister Artium Zoltan Paskowiak was extended by chapters named Bela **Bartók**, *Otto Wels* and *Carlo Schmidt*. "How can someone attempt to write a historical novel, a hymn to the FRG, perhaps even intending to create German literature, and leave out these important personalities?" Dr. Neugebauer muttered to himself ...

So, he continued to read:

"Mr. Nietzsche, this text is a disgrace, I don't think you will find any publisher willing to print it. How many publishing houses did you approach before ours?" "Nine," Nietzsche answered sadly.

"You could self-publish your book. This is not popular literature. However, with a printing cost subsidy, we would be willing to print your pamphlet. Not a large print run, but perhaps someone, somewhere, will enjoy your text. How many parts is your Zarathustra to consist of?" the publisher asked suspiciously. "Four parts are planned," Nietzsche said crossly. "How many copies of the manuscript do you have?" "I am in possession of two copies of the first part of the manuscript," Nietzsche replied bitterly. "Then leave one with me, and I'll take it to my co-editor for a second opinion." "All right!" Nietzsche exclaimed and briskly left the publisher's office.

*

Hans Massler had been a publisher for 40 years. He knew only too well what kind of literature would sell. With a literacy rate of 75% in the German Reich, songbooks, cookbooks, prayer books sold quite well. Trashy, low-brow novels were big sellers. You could always sell a Karl May. But this? Zarathustra? An oriental theme? "Who would subject his brain to such convolutions? The proclamation of a bitter egomaniac who seemed close to madness. To claim that God is dead ... an affront to every good Catholic ... In ten years' time, Friedrich Nietzsche would more likely be forgotten because nobody had read him, rather than achieving any kind of economic relevance and then be forgotten. Was this Nietzsche trying to become a Schopenhauer? A Ludwig Feuerbach? But the good Feuerbach was unique within the German Empire. He had died barely a decade before." "Hah!" the publisher declared. "A Nietzsche? A would-be Feuerbach, what a presumption! But business is business, we will print this blasphemous work, perhaps someone will read it and enjoy it ... Nietzsche - a Ludwig Feuerbach!" Stunned, Massler shook his mottled gray head.

*

Friedrich Nietzsche opened the publisher's large envelope. He pulled out his manuscript and a letter.

Dear Mr. Nietzsche!

After consultation with my co-publisher, we have decided to refrain from printing your Zarathustra, Part One, as a self-published manuscript with printing cost subsidy.

Yours sincerely

Hans Massler

Nietzsche took the manuscript and angrily threw it against the wall. It came to lie next to the armchair. "You monkeys," he shouted. "Must your ears be smashed so that you learn to hear with your eyes? You will erect monuments to me yet!!!"

*

Nietzsche provisionally packed his suitcases and went down to the reception of the boarding house where he was currently staying. "Order a carriage for me and have my suitcases brought down," he said to the man at the reception desk. "With pleasure, sir," the receptionist replied. After a few minutes, a young boy came down with his suitcases and said: "Herr Nietzsche, there is another manuscript on the floor in your room, I didn't know what to do with it, so I just left it there. Shall I fetch it for you?" Nietzsche cried out in disenchantment: "No, burn it, I know it by heart!" And ran out to the carriage.

*

"The only interesting thing about Mr. Paskowiak's entire book is probably the fact that, running through it as a common thread, are the achievements of Prince von Bismarck," Dr. Neugebauer mused.

Dr. Neugebauer added a note at the end:

EDITING ENDS.

He looked at the list of chapters that had been edited to the end: Ernst Heinrich Wilhelm Stephan, Werner von Siemens, Richard Strauß, Ernst Jünger in World War I, The Treaties of Rapallo 1922, Alfred Döblin, Walther Rathenau. He quickly skimmed the speech of Otto Wels, a member of parliament, on the Enabling Act of 1933 with the heavily historical quote "Freedom and life can be taken from us, honor cannot," and again skimmed the edited chapters Ernst Reuter, Carlo Schmidt, Konrad Adenauer, Munich Olympics, Reunification. He probably had to come up with something else for the preface and the epilogue. The original version didn't work at all. At that moment, the phone rang. The display read: Paskowiak. The editor took the call and said: "Zoltan ..." but before he could even utter a greeting, the caller began to sputter: "Harald, hello, I don't want to rush you, but I have to publish my book. I'm extremely pressed for time ... How far along are you with the editing?"

CUSTOMIZE AUSTRIAN ACCENT

"In principle, I would say that I am now finished with the proofreading," Dr. Neugebauer replied in his typical tone of voice with its distinctive Styrian dialect tinge. "The epilogue I would still like to rewrite, and the scenes when the reunited German Olympic team marches into the stadium in Albertville. And I'm thinking of mentioning German President Richard von Weizsäcker, whose eyes were watering at that moment. That's patriotism, my good man." "I see," Paskowiak replied. "Yes, that's good, that's very good ... yes, do that, insert that as well. And switch back to High German," Paskowiak laughed, "we are in Prussia here, ha-haha." "Thank you, mon ami, you are truly the literary man of the hour ..."

"How about sushi? Shall we have a sushi dinner on Wednesday?" Paskowiak asked casually. "How about a Strammer Max and a beer?" Dr. Neugebauer returned the question. "Falafel, sushi, eating out anywhere in Berlin is just too ethnic for me nowadays. We should have a Leberkäs and enjoy a beer with it and finish it off with a cappuccino." "Fine," Paskowiak said. "See you Wednesday then? Five p.m. at Café Hardenberg?" "Yes, that's good," Dr. Neugebauer ended the conversation, "see you Wednesday."

*

The confused text with the grandiloquent title IMPERIUM MAGNUM INFERNALIS had been sent to Dr. Neugebauer via Henriette by a Turk who seemed to be even more confused than his manuscript. This very modest "work of the century" was a shallow, trashy novel. "Well, the Turks tend not to be a great literary people," Dr. Harald Neugebauer thought. At least this one could manage to get something down on paper. Henriette had brought the Turk to him to apply a little stylistic polishing to his debut novel. But it was trash literature at its best. "What could a Turk possibly have to convey to the world through a novel?" Dr. Neugebauer asked himself and began to read the manuscript again:

"I'd rather be somewhere in the Caribbean ordering grilled fish Creole style. How about a grilled catfish instead of fish and chips?" She was speaking to her visibly younger companion, who nodded in agreement, pitch-black braid hanging down over her chest. The Indian woman in a yellow sari listened to her silently, interested.

"Oui, how about a Cajun-style catfish - les Cadiens?" the old lady asked, smiling. "The secret of a Creole or Cajun-style barbecue catfish is not to use garlic powder. Instead, the garlic cloves are pressed several times through a garlic press until they are a homogeneous paste. Also, the bulbs should be pureed and drained. Only connoisseurs know that garlic should be crushed, not cut, to preserve its flavors." "It's one thing to pull a standard recipe from the net," the old lady added, instinctively grabbing her parietal lobe interface on the left side of her head. The red glowing diode indicated that it was off. The lady, who was a good sixty years older than her companion, looked at the woman in her mid-thirties whose black eyes were distinguished by a deep, penetrating gaze. Despite her sandals, she tried to keep up with the haggard old African woman. "Preparing a Cajun-style barbecue catfish is a meditative process. Of course, in this ritual, we pick off the parsley leaves, one at a time, delicately and leaf by leaf, rather than chopping them roughly with a knife. And of course, the cayenne pepper is freshly ground by us, as is the black pepper, which we also grind ourselves. I personally prefer black pepper from Albania. I believe the highest quality pepper in the world grows in Albania. But the cayenne pepper, of course, comes from West Africa. We call it pilli-pilli. Have you ever tried pilli-pilli, my dear?" The old lady spoke to the Indian woman who was a head taller than her and looked down at her. The younger woman bent her neck back and raised her head, indicating "no." The old woman responded with a smile. "I still have to get used to the fact that in India a nod means no and a shake of the head to the right and left means yes. Pilli-pilli is the highest quality cayenne pepper available, so ideally it should be part of the real catfish recipe. The butter we use should be unsalted Irish butter. To top everything off, we use homemade sea salt. After stirring fresh Turkish oregano and fresh Turkish thyme through all the ingredients, we puree everything again by hand with a mortar in a ceramic bowl. Then we let everything stand for about 45 minutes so that the essences can mix. To grill catfish, it is essential to skin the fish. This is because fish not only breathe through their gills, but also filter water through their skin, which is called transpiration. For this reason, the skin of a fish contains harmful waste substances. We use the same principle when we turn a human into a zombie by transferring the puffer fish's nerve toxin tetrodotoxin to the victim through the skin. In most cases, all it takes is a whiff of the poison powder blown from the palm of your hand. The gloves you wear should be made of thick plastic. Vaudou haïtien, my dear. The system of transpiration is similar to osmosis in plants. After we skin the fish, and before we rub the fish with the spice mixture, here comes my secret recipe. A small amount of cornmeal is now used to coat the fish. The best way to do this is to press the fish into the cornmeal and then rub the spice mixture onto the cornmeal coated fish. After that, you can fry the fish in butter for about three minutes. Be careful not to breathe in the spice fumes." The old lady paused for a moment, smiled pensively, and then continued: "I'm writing a book, a book for gourmets. A collection of special recipes from around the globe." She waxed rapturously. "The first time I ate the real catfish creole was in Port-au-Prince, in Haiti in 1967," the old lady reminisced, sinking into her thoughts. "It was the year of the zombie plague in Haiti. I had dinner at the Section communale Croix-des-Missions with a member of the Tonton Macoutes, where catfish créole was served to me for the first time in that particular way. I was so delighted with the meal that I bribed the chef to tell me the recipe." She smiled thoughtfully and curiously asked the Indian woman, "Do you know the Tonton Macoutes?" The latter again replied in the negative with a nod. "We had a bottle of Haitian rum from the local rum distillery. You must know, Haitian rum is very famous among connoisseurs. The Tonton Macoutes militia was the feared paramilitary secret police of the president of Haiti, Papa Doc Duvalier. A colonel of the Tonton Macoutes invited me to dinner; his name was Josué, a charmer through and through. And we enjoyed catfish with a bottle of rum. I was much younger and naïve at the time and was on a study tour. My trip to Haiti had come about through many private contacts and sponsors. Josué was my tour guide, so to speak. We visited a zombie plantation in Haiti." The Indian woman regarded the old woman with curiosity, eyes shining. The old woman returned her gaze. "You must know, my dear, the leaders of the Tonton Macoutes were all voodoo priests. Tetrodotoxin was unknown in the West at that time. During those years, the Tonton Macoutes produced zombies nonstop. The Tonton Macoutes turned every one of the political opposition who could not escape into zombies using the nerve agent. The zombies then worked on secret plantations as zombie slaves. This nerve agent makes the victim appear clinically dead, but the brain is still active. The victim is buried as presumed dead, but his senses still function. After being buried for several hours, the victim is dug up again and the antidote is administered. However, the lack of oxygen to the brain has already left irreparable damage, resulting in micromotor dysfunction in the musculoskeletal system and damage to the corpus striatum in the brain. This is the reason why zombies move so awkwardly." Then she laughed out loud and continued speaking. "Occasionally, it happened that the victims' memory fragments caused them, years later, to leave the plantation when they suddenly felt the urge to go home. I would have loved to see people's faces when a dead person, after two or three years as a zombie, suddenly reappeared on their own doorstep ..." She looked at the Indian woman, and said: "Here we are ..."

*

So that was the co-author of Henriette's book. He put aside the Turk's literary garbage, went to the microwave, and heated the meatloaf that had been in the refrigerator for several days. He thought about the Ottoman, who was, after all, so different. The Levant, or rather what was left of the Levant, the Orient in fact. A crudely carved perpetrator people who had subjugated all and everyone and made them pay tribute, even the Americans back in Libya. After all, they had their empire, of whose myth the Ottoman still lived. And today? The former fez-wearer was domesticated by Atatürk. But somehow that went wrong, too, as we can see in Berlin, he thought to himself. Yes, the Turk; what kind of symbiotic love-hate relationship was it they had with the Turks? The hard worker who had been brought in from Anatolia in the 1960s by the German government to generate the economic miracle in post-war Germany. That was 60 years ago now. The Italian, the Portuguese, the Spaniard left again. The Turk stayed and increased by mitosis; logarithmically. Of course, it was just another myth that workers were requested from Turkey - many things in Germany were based on mythmaking. He put the third bottle of Köstritzer beer on the table and remembered: "Dispatches of the German embassy in Ankara from that time showed: The Turks, the heroes of the Korean War, forced the USA to put pressure on the Federal Republic of Germany, so that Turkey could send workers to Germany, in order to be able to transfer by means of the guest workers urgently needed foreign currency to the homeland. Be that as it may ... they were then received with open arms, just like the urgently needed dentists and engineers some time later, who invaded Western Europe in an epic migration, as it were, just as Goth engineers and dentists had invaded the Roman Empire before. The archaic social competence of the Saracen fascinated him. There is something definitive about it, he thought, like Nietzsche, something like philosophizing with a hammer, the only difference being, without philosophy and without Nietzsche ... Dr.

Neugebauer laughed contritely as he thought of the asylum seekers from Fiji who were now settled in Berlin. But his favorite story was still that of the Somali pirates. If Ephraim Kishon had been German, he would certainly have written a book about it ... and would have been excommunicated from German society, alongside Thilo Sarrazin. Actually, come to think of it, what had become of the dozen pirates? They had hijacked a German merchant ship with speedboats off the Somali coast. After their arrest, the pirates were brought to Germany to stand trial. Of course, they all applied for political asylum in Germany at that time, which was granted to them immediately ... including family reunion ... Because no one will be deported to a country where civil war is raging. Germany well appreciates proactivity ... These politniks, he thought, what exactly are these self-promoters debating? The Foreigners' Registration Office in Berlin had been secretly renamed Immigration Office without anyone noticing. He raised his bottle of Köstritzer in an imaginary toast to Schopenhauer, grinning sarcastically as he thought of his words: "All our evil comes from the fact that we cannot be alone ..."

*

"How about that?" exclaimed Zoltan, "An indigenous man was elected president in Bolivia yesterday. His name is Evo Morales, he represents the coca farmers." Henriette replied: "Oh, politics don't interest me much ..." and poked at her tuna salad, which she was enjoying with some freshly squeezed orange juice. As usual, Café Hardenberg was packed with students from Berlin's Technical University. Zoltan waited impatiently for his toast, which, he felt, was taking a long time. "I guess there are more important things going on than an Indian in politics," she said. Zoltan slightly raised his right eyebrow and asked with an amused undertone: "Well, Ms. Cultural Luminary, like what?" "We have," she replied with somewhat preening indignation, "the 150th anniversary of the death of the poet Heinrich Heine, the 50th anniversary of the death of Berthold Brecht, and the Ibsen Year ... so the new year 2006 is an important year from the point of view of literature. Zoltan, it's a good thing you're a man of letters, otherwise I'd think you were more interested in politics than literature ..." Slightly dejected, Zoltan replied: "I was not aware of the Ibsen year. Nordic literature is not exactly my métier." He gazed at the beautiful face of a woman in her late twenties, a strong character, an accomplished legal professional. Henriette could easily be mistaken for the

Italian-American actress Isabella Rossellini. Zoltan had never been able to decide whether to fall in love with her eyes or with her intellect. So then he decided to fall in love with both. "My delicate muse," he said, "reach out to me with your delicate, piano-tested hands." He took her hand and kissed her long, graceful fingers. Henriette looked into Zoltan's blue eyes and blushed slightly. She didn't like demonstrating closeness in public. She had never been able to get used to that. They both knew they would soon be talking about getting married. "When are we going to visit your parents again, Henriette?" Zoltan asked. "This weekend my parents invited us to dinner. My father is crazy about you. He sustained an injury in his right shoulder during World War II, in the Sudetenland. Ever since I told him about your family background, he's been blown away by you. You have all the aces up your sleeve with him. I find it impossible, this German posturing. I told him that he should move to Osnabrück so that he could live near the Teutoburg Forest and indulge his German heritage. Race consciousness is a terrible thing." "Well, I was only born in Czechoslovakia, but grew up in Vienna, as you know, so in that respect I don't have much to do with the Sudetenland, at least sociologically." He did not indulge her argument any further and left it at that. In the garden of Café Hardenberg, the outdoor heaters were burning, as usual. The crowded garden space was covered with umbrellas that offered rudimentary protection from the wet air. Silence reigned between them for a few seconds, and Zoltan lost himself in his beloved Henriette's eyes, when a man walked by on the sidewalk, talking loudly on the phone in a foreign language. The distinctive noisy gibberish, which appeared to be Turkish, was interspersed with vulgar expletives in German. Any outsiders would basically be able to understand only the loud, obscene insults. Those guests of the café who were closest to the passing man, demonstratively gave the resulting unpleasant and embarrassing situation the silent treatment. "Well, well," Zoltan said with a condescending undertone. "An Ali Baba, another specimen of the libido-driven enricher of our culture," and laughed contemptuously. He followed this with a quote by Hartman von Aue: "If the other puts up with him, all quarrels are settled ..." However, the laughter stuck in his throat, for tragically, the man, seeing the two of them in the café garden, walked directly towards Henriette and Zoltan. He interrupted his phone call and called out in a bright, sympathetic voice: "Hello Miss Frohwein!!!" Astonished, Henriette replied: "Hello Alpaslan!" Puzzled and perplexed, Zoltan observed the situation, and when the man with the long, braided hair, an elongated mustache, and the strange name of Alpaslan greeted Zoltan with a "Good day to you, too, sir," the latter gave an irritated nod of the head that was meant to imply a return greeting. Zoltan thought to himself that this must be how one imagines an ancient warrior from the steppes would look. "Really good to see you, Miss Frohwein, you are the best lawyer in the world. Thank you! You have helped me so much, if you ever need any help, no matter what, you must call me. Here, take my phone number, wait, I'll write it down for you." He rummaged in his pockets and said: "My phone number has changed. I'll just write it on another business card. " Alpaslan handed Henriette a blank turquoise business card on which he wrote his number. On the back was an American phone number and next to it in parentheses was Skype. There was something written underneath the American number that Henriette did not understand. She replied: "Thank you Alpaslan. It's my job to help you. After all, I am a criminal defense lawyer," and smiled mischievously at Alpaslan. "But don't you need the American phone number anymore?" "It can't hurt if you have it as well," he said somewhat cryptically, adding a "ha-haha." Alpaslan turned to Zoltan: "Man, the woman is a precious pearl, a diamond, marry her. And take good care of her!" He laughed loudly, then noisily said goodbye and departed, leaving behind a smiling Henriette and a puzzled Zoltan.

*

When the editor sat down at his desk again, he decided to spend a little time on Henriette's text. With rare exceptions, Dr. Neugebauer avoided proofreading legal books. This was not because he was not able to, but because a legal treatise had no entertainment value, especially since the legal work of Henriette Paskowiak, a graduate of the Free University of Berlin, who lectured on the Ali-Baba Redneck and Aggro-Turk, seemed to be entirely obsolete from a sociological perspective. What could have possessed this soul to write a legal treatise on the Osman? Germany, a mosaic of cultures ... That would have me run for the hills, thought Dr. Neugebauer. As he opened a bottle of dark Köstritzer beer, he pondered his own existence and whispered to himself: "I ... I suppose I must be a venal hack." But that was the spirit of the age in Germany, he thought ... He raised the bottle as in a symbolic toast and said: "Sovietsky Soyuz ... perished, but reanimated in Merkel's Germany ..." Then he bent over the manuscript with the title:

"Application Methodology and Game-Theoretic Modeling of Cultural Ethnocide and Minority Rights Litigations."

Applied strategy analysis for linguistic rights in transnational linguistic minority litigations.

A case study of the Turkish language in the European Union

"Hmm..." Disgruntled, Dr. Neugebauer read on and skimmed through the text:

According to the Constitution of the Republic of Cyprus, the official languages of the Republic of Cyprus are Greek and Turkish. The Republic of Cyprus has been a member of the European Union since May 1, 2004. The preamble to the Treaty on European Union states that the Treaty "...rests on the cultural, religious and humanist heritage of Europe" and reaffirms its commitment "to the principles of liberty, democracy and respect for human rights." The Treaty on European Union (TEU) emphasizes respect for human rights and non-discrimination, while stating that the EU should respect "the richness of its cultural and linguistic diversity." The Treaty on the Functioning of the European Union (TFEU) emphasizes that the Union's action shall pursue the following objectives: "To develop the European dimension in education, in particular through the teaching and dissemination of the languages of the Member States" while fully respecting cultural and linguistic diversity. The

Charter of Fundamental Rights of the EU prohibits discrimination on the grounds of language and obliges the Union to respect linguistic diversity. Every citizen of the Union has the right to address an EU institution or body in any of these languages and to receive a reply in the same language. According to the regulation, the EU institutions currently have 25 official and working languages. The Maltese and Luxembourgish languages, among others, are excluded. It is possible to correspond with any European Union institution in the 25 official national languages within the European Union. Not included are Frisian, Mirandese, Galician, Occitan, Catalan, and Basque. The respective populations in the Netherlands, Portugal and Spain are 100% bilingual. Among others, the population of Malta (514,564) is 100% bilingual (Maltese and English). The population of Luxembourg (626,108) is also 100% bilingual (Luxembourgish and French). The nationals of Malta and Luxembourg are able to correspond with the institutions of the European Union in their national languages (English and French). Since the population of the Republic of Cyprus is not de facto bilingual - the estimated population is 1,213,380, of which 326,000 are non-Greek speakers - non-Greek speakers are not given the opportunity to correspond in their language with the EU institutions, which is enshrined as a fundamental right in the Constitution of the Republic of Cyprus. There are at least 10 Member States in the European Union with significant Turkish bilingual communities. Many Turkish-speaking EU citizens are not advanced speakers of their national language within the European Union. Dr. Neugebauer laughed out loud. "Other than a handful of long-assimilated Turks, can any of them speak German at all?" He read on indignantly ... Therefore, a possibility for written communication with the institutions of the European Union does not exist for this population group. According to the European Convention on Human Rights, enshrined in Article 14, any discrimination related to language is prohibited, even if it is negligent. For said reasons, this fundamental right can be claimed under Article 21(1) and Article 22 of the CHARTER OF FUNDAMENTAL RIGHTS OF THE EUROPEAN UNION (2012/C 326/02) and under Article 14 of the European Convention on Human Rights. Moreover, according to the Universal Declaration of Human Rights, Article 2, and the Universal Declaration of Language Rights, the speakers of the Turkish official language in the European Union, which is enshrined in the Constitution of the Republic of Cyprus, have the right to write and receive a reply in Turkish - to and from any institution of the EU - in addition to the 25 official languages.

If this right, which is enshrined in the fundamental rights of the EU, does not apply or is not applicable upon request according to the regulations and laws of the European Union, it would be necessary in this case to legally present which paragraph of the regulations and laws of the European Union is violated by the recognition of the Turkish language as an official and working language of the European Union and why the Turkish language is not protected by the European Convention on Human Rights, as enshrined in Article 14 ...

Dr. Neugebauer thought for a moment and began to gaze out of the window. Now he understood why the Turkish co-author of the book, who was also the author of the trash novel, did not want to be named. He was simply afraid of a sudden pulmonary embolism ...

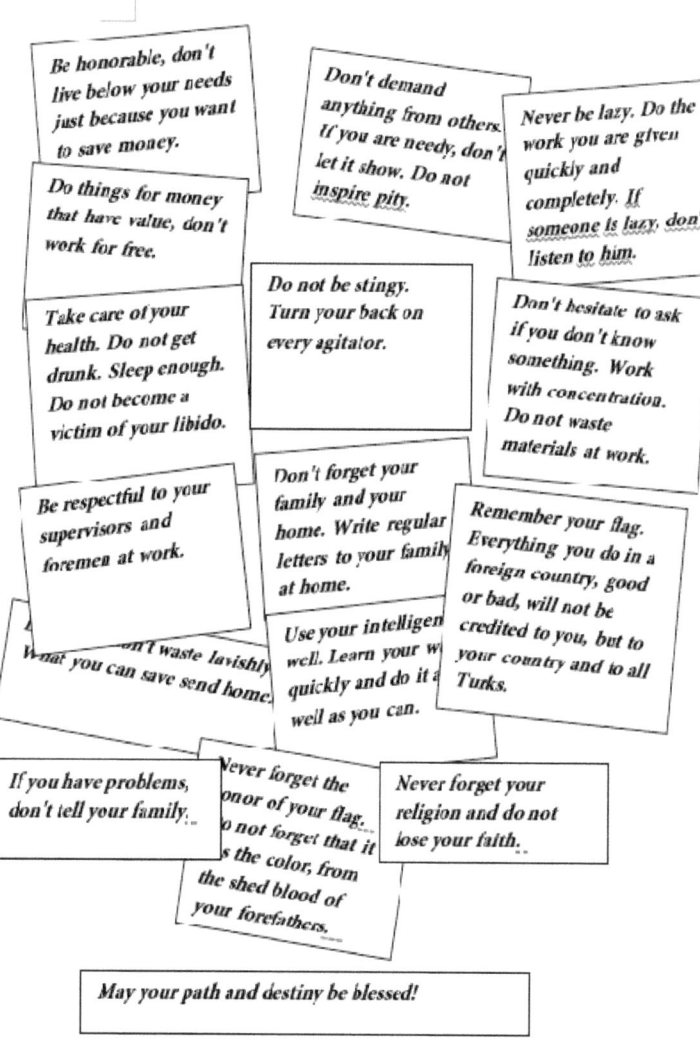

Be honorable, don't live below your needs just because you want to save money.

Don't demand anything from others. If you are needy, don't let it show. Do not inspire pity.

Never be lazy. Do the work you are given quickly and completely. If someone is lazy, don't listen to him.

Do things for money that have value, don't work for free.

Do not be stingy. Turn your back on every agitator.

Don't hesitate to ask if you don't know something. Work with concentration. Do not waste materials at work.

Take care of your health. Do not get drunk. Sleep enough. Do not become a victim of your libido.

Be respectful to your supervisors and foremen at work.

Don't forget your family and your home. Write regular letters to your family at home.

Remember your flag. Everything you do in a foreign country, good or bad, will not be credited to you, but to your country and to all Turks.

...on't waste lavishly. What you can save send home.

Use your intelligen... well. Learn your w... quickly and do it a... well as you can.

If you have problems, don't tell your family...

Never forget the honor of your flag... Do not forget that it is the color, from the shed blood of your forefathers.

Never forget your religion and do not lose your faith...

May your path and destiny be blessed!

ONURLU OL

- Para biriktireceğim diye gerektiğinden aşağı bir şekilde yaşama
- Kimseden öteberi isteme. Muhtaç olsan da belli etme.
- Kendine başkalarını acındırma.
- Parayla olacak işleri parasız yapmağa kalkışma.
- Cimrilik etme.
- Kışkırtıcılara sırtını çevir.

ZEKANI İYİ KULLAN

- İşini çabuk öğren ve en iyi şekilde yap.
- Bilmediğini sormaktan çekinme.
- Dikkatsizlik edip işinde malzeme zayiatına sebep olma.
- Tembellik etme. Verilen işi tam zamanında noksansız bitir.
- Boş ver diyene uyma.
- İşyerinde idarecilere, ustalara saygı göster.

AİLENİ, EVİNİ UNUTMA

- Evine muntazam mektup yaz, merak ettirme.
- Sıkıntılarını ailene yazma.
- Tutumlu ol. Paranı sokağa atma. Artırabildiğini evine gönder.

SAĞLIĞINI KORU

- Kendine iyi bak.
- Sarhoş olma.
- Uyku saatinde uyu.
- Uçkuruna sahip ol.

YOLUN
VE
BAHTIN
AÇIK OLSUN

BAYRAĞINI DÜŞÜN

- Yabancı ilde yapacağın iyi iş de kötü iş de şahsına yüklenmez. Türklüğe ait olur.
- Bayrağının şerefini hatırından çıkarma. Rengini atalarının dökülen kanından aldığını unutma.
- Dinden imandan ayrılma.

"Not only is the Turk not capable of being integrated but now he also wants rights," Dr. Neugebauer mused and said: "In Berlin one already feels as though one is among donkeys and camels." He would correct and adjust the slant of this pamphlet schemingly written by someone from the murky political left. What had Paskowiak been thinking when he married such a woman?! ... And their marriage had lasted 16 years already. Dr. Neugebauer thought ... The agenda of the scheming left and that of the hegemonic authorities was clear. United by diversity ad nauseam, German society was to be put into an anarchic state by over-individualization and excessive amoral-hedonistic decadence. Eat - Fuck - Watch TV, those were the catchwords ... The political center no longer existed. Society as depicted in the media had moved so far to the left that cultural self-denigration of national identity became a duty. Everything else, by definition, was considered right-wing ... The terror imposed on German society by the left-wing fascists, he thought sadly ... Where this would lead was clearly foreseeable. Angka - Pol Pot's Angka. Cambodian left-wing fascism at its best. Everybody who dared to wonder out loud, Cui bono? was immediately hit around the head with the Nazi cudgel - the political-psychological killer argument, the intellectual castration of the German people who had been re-educated in the best social-anthropological manner ... Well, such thoughts were probably Orwellian thought crimes and a double-false way of thinking ... in the German Potcmkin state of democracy simulation. At what point would the Basic Law Article 20 (4) actually come into effect, he asked himself ... and took a few peanuts and threw them into his mouth. "Shaize Doischlaan," he imitated the Berlin-Turkish term for the German state. He raised his Köstritzer beer and said: "You too are Doishlaan, Osman," and took a large swig. And thought about what had gone wrong in Germany a long time ago when, in the days of Helmut Kohl, the Turk still seemed to be integrated and even spoke German. But today? The multiculti agenda of the green fascists with the slogan Germany is abolishing itself, and that's a good thing, had culturally atomized society and likewise conditioned a new Turk, who now appears as the Turkish-Islamic fundamentalized welfare recipient, who idly, day after day, shuffles thoughts back and forth – if he can formulate any ideas at all, since for lack of education he has neither an adequate command of the Turkish nor the German language and communicates in both languages only rudimentarily with a vocabulary of 300 words and phrases. Inertly apolitical and paralyzed within the Harz IV benefit system that provides barely enough to keep body and soul together, sitting out his life. Hush money. Miserably cultureless, not belonging to any culture, vegetating in a vulgar way, both reassimilated in and disintegrated from German society. If the Turk is a victim and so are we Germans, then, he wondered, who is the perpetrator? "A pulmonary embolism question," he said out loud to himself. He stopped such thoughts, slammed the manuscript shut, got up from the table and went out onto the balcony to look at the street ...

A day later, he couldn't help but think about the pulmonary embolism question again. He went back to his desk and opened the manuscript by Henriette and her co-author, the Trash Turk, at a random page, and started reading: Turkish and Turkish-speaking societies have unclaimed rights in the European Union. The reason why these rights are not claimed, and cannot be claimed, is that the European Union and the Western alliance see this as a geostrategic axiom. According to the Ariel Sharon government, the number of Muslims living in the European Union who will have the right to vote will increase rapidly in the coming years, and they (the member countries of the European Union) concluded that the voting rights of such masses have a very high potential to influence the foreign policy of the European Union. For that reason, the EU leadership has decided to apply the Coudenhove-Kalergi Plan on an intellectual basis to Turks, in order to neutralize the Turkish intellectual elite in the European Community through social engineering and intellectual ethnocide and to prevent their formation into an intelligentsia. Moreover, the path of cultural ethnocide and moral degradation has been chosen and is being applied to all Turkish and Muslim societies. In terms of the application of ethnocide, individuals have technically been victims of denationalization and deculturalization through the absorption of Turkish culture, which has not been replaced by any other cultural context. Turks live in a South African Bantustan of apartheid, by name of "Berliner Kiez". Then again, the repolarization of Turkish society and its value system in the European Union is systematically achieved by imposing forced precarization on the great masses of Anatolian origin through film and television. For example, films like "Against the Wall" and "Four Blocks" create an intrinsic motivation in which false role models are psychologically implanted in the Muslim minorities as their primary orientation. The same principle is also applied by the music industry, e.g. with corresponding song lyrics. The equivalent for young Germans is film titles such as "Fuck you, Goethe", an affront to the most significant representative of the German Age of Reason, the symbol of German literature par excellence. This is intended to keep the German youth living in Germany away from the ideal of the Age of Reason and German culture and its roots. For example, the nephew of marketing expert Edward Bernays is now the CEO of the Netflix channel. Bernays' uncle, by contrast, was Dr. Sigmund Freud. False role models are deliberately created. Islam, on the other hand, is being steered toward alternative paths. Thus, in the EU, sectarian phenomena that do not exist or are marginal in the Orient appear to represent broad Islamic masses. Edward Bernays' marketing techniques have been used to shape Muslim minorities, especially Turkish society. They have been primarily constructed in the media as the antithesis of the Occident, the Western states of Europe. Similarly, Turks and Muslims living in the European Union have become the absolute victims of Zbigniew Brzezinski's theory of "tittytainment". For example, the highest density of slot machines and gambling machines in Germany is found in districts dominated by Turkish and Arab populations.

An expert report commissioned by the German Federal Government, excerpted here, states:

Scientific Services of the German Bundestag

Criteria for the recognition of national minorities

Elaboration WD 3 - 3000 -067/09

Completion of the work: March 24, 2009

Department WD 3: Constitution and
Administration

1. criteria for the recognition of national minorities

The federal government considers groups of the population as national minorities that meet the following 5 criteria:

a) Their relatives are German citizens,

b) they differ from the majority people by their own language, culture and history, i.e. their own identity,

c) they want to preserve this identity,

d) they are traditionally native to Germany,

e) they live here in ancestral settlement areas.

For example, a party representing ~~Turks with German citizenship would~~ not benefit from the minority privilege, as this group of persons is not considered to be **traditionally native to** *Germany and to be living here in* **ancestral settlement areas.**

According to the International Law => E/CN.4/Sub.2/384/Rev.1, para. 568., minorities are defined as follows: "A group numerically inferior to the rest of the population of a State, in a non-dominant position, whose members - as nationals of the State - have ethnic, religious or linguistic characteristics different from those of the rest of the population and who show, even if only by implication, a sense of solidarity based on the preservation of their culture, traditions, religion or language. "

The EDITOR: * wrong word choice, => GG§116. (1) "German is, who possesses German nationality"!

Kimberly: It is a quote from the expert opinion, I cannot change it!

Annex; 150 EX/37

GENERAL DECLARATION ON THE RIGHTS OF LANGUAGES - TITLE - United Nations Concept

"This Declaration considers a language community to be any human community historically located in a particular territorial space, whether or not that space is recognized, that identifies itself as a people and has developed a common language as a natural means of communication and cultural cohesion among its members."

If German reunification is a historical fact, so is the influx of Turkish guest workers into

Germany. Until reunification, Turkish guest workers were only allowed to settle in specific districts that had been allocated to them. The following was stamped in their Turkish passports: "Not permitted to settle outside the districts of Neukölln and Kreuzberg". Children of first-generation Turks born in Berlin-Neukölln and Kreuzberg are Germans under law, as most of them received citizenship through naturalization. They also possess German state identification documents. The third generation, who were born in these districts, are second generation Germans, and are, according to international law, a community historically located in a specific territorial area.

While German expert opinion speaks of "traditional", international law defines it as "historical".

Raphael Lemkin, the initiator of Human Rights, divided the Nazi ethnocide program into different areas. He distinguished political, cultural, economic, social, physical, biological, religious, and moral ethnocide. Under the heading "cultural", Lemkin detailed various measures that he considered part of cultural ethnocide. The first measure is the prohibition of the use of a group's own language in schools and printing presses. The Nazis enforced teaching according to National Socialist principles and created vocational schools. In Poland, Polish youths were forbidden to participate in humanities studies because they might develop "independent national Polish thought". Instead, the youths of undesirable groups were sent to vocational schools to become skilled workers for German industry.

In the federal state of Berlin, a different path was chosen to disguise the cultural ethnocide that was gradually implemented after the Helmut Kohl era. The requirements for the Abitur examinations were gradually lowered. The lowered requirements meant that many foreigners who would not have been able to pass the Abitur in the federal state of Bavaria, for example, were able to pass in Berlin. Thus, the statistics were fudged. This means that it is now very easy for foreigners with a low standard of education to pass the Abitur examination in Berlin. At University level, however, the failure rate is exorbitantly high. Therefore, the dropout rate among foreigners and Germans with a migration background is high compared to the native German population. Furthermore, every high school graduate has to master English and another foreign language in addition to German. The second elective language can be any language, depending on what the school offers. However, Turkish is not included in the languages offered, or to a very limited extent only. A Turkish high school graduate from an educationally disadvantaged family who grew up with rudimentary Turkish has to learn German, English and another foreign language, i.e., three foreign languages, while native speakers of German only have to master two foreign languages to successfully pass the Abitur. Someone without adequate command of the native language is not able to formulate differentiated chains of thoughts, let alone learn foreign languages effectively in their entirety. This Orwellian language modification, systematically applied in the federal state of Berlin, has resulted in today's forty-five to fifty-five-year-old Turks speaking German and Turkish far better than those born after 1995.

In relation to the European-Turkish communities, there are natural alliances and contrasts in this regard. The subject of this methodological research is the analysis of the roadmap to the "Pan-European Congress of the Turkish Minority". It is an investigation of the social, social-anthropological, geostrategic, economic, diplomatic, and legal dimensions of the European Congress of the Turkish Minority (ATAK-Avrupa Türk Azinliklar Kurultayi), which will inevitably gain increasing importance in the European Community in future decades.

Dr. Neugebauer was speechless ... Stunned, he tried to reconstruct what he was reading ... What was that Turk up to? Was he trying to establish a Mameluke state on EU soil or maybe assert minority rights? Did public international law even permit such a thing? Why did a Henriette Paskowiak even participate in the formulation of these ideas? The Turks were doing well in the EU – relatively speaking. They were able to do business without restriction and live in their chosen biotopes ... most of them were uneducated and a little more than aggro ... but ... Hmm. Did the EU Turk even have the intellectual capacity to pull something like that off??? He thought for a moment ... Then he said: There are only four possibilities:

The Islamic minorities will eventually start to organize and achieve a "de facto" minority status within the European Union through religion or language.
We attract them into mainstream society and integrate them, as we managed to do up until the end of the Helmut Kohl era, when the Turk did not stand out in the street even by his clothes and appearance, and include these people into the community and the culture of Europe, into mainstream society, on an equal footing.
We send everyone away again to all the corners of the earth whence they came, by mass

deprivation of citizenship, disregarding any special right of abode status.

No, the fourth option, that's not an option ...

*

Every so often, Zoltan would approach Dr. Neugebauer with texts written by dubious people. Such as right now, with a text by a "friend" ... Naturally, another one of those pulmonary-embolism candidates, as Dr. Harald Neugebauer liked to put it ... He opened a random chapter:

... In the 1950s, the initiation of the conceptual arts was anthropologically imposed on Western societies by the Western alliance in a gradual manner. All essential art forms had already been displaced by it. The aim transmitted here was that everything was considered art, and anyone who wanted to, could be an artist. The intention behind this was to modify the concept of aesthetics and to grind down the cultural strongholds: Film, music, fiction, pictorial representation. Anything capable of profaning perception was perpetually integrated into art in accordance with classical conditioning according to Pavlov. There will no longer be a Shakespearean actor like Sir Laurence Olivier, nor a Van Gogh; instead, people with a profane understanding of art will be used as multipliers.

The Professor of Art now installs balloons that are powered by propellers and rise and fall in the air – promotion guaranteed! A domestic pig vomits against a canvas and a monkey dumps paint over it; this is conceptual art. The painting now sells for a million euros. Art for art's sake no longer exists; art is now a monetary consumer product. Everything obscene and debased becomes acceptable and graffiti applied with a grease marker is equal to Botticelli and rap is equal to Beethoven. Conceptual art is the most profane of all the pedagogical art forms. However, along with music, film serves as the foundation of educational methodology. This is how we can tell that film is the most strategically relevant educational methodology: If we don't pay for electricity or water, these services are very soon disconnected by the utility companies. By contrast, should we refuse to pay for television and radio, reception will not be cut off, but we will go to jail ...

A sample manuscript for a sitcom:

Apartment living room - at the table

Two people are playing chess and smoking a joint.

A man continuously pukes his guts out into a plastic bucket. He wears glasses; a paper napkin is stuck underneath the glass over his right eye. No one pays him any attention.

The two chess players are totally immersed in their game – a man with a pointed hat made of tinfoil, and a heavily made-up Chinese transvestite in drag. In the background an old Chinese woman sits in an armchair, looks toward an aquarium and giggles to herself.

Grandma: "Ooh, shit."

Continues in Chinese:

"Zhi shi tai hao le."

Continuous:

"The monkey king yes, yes, that was the monkey king."

A rolled-up carpet lies on the floor with a person in it who is not moving. The man with the tinfoil hat is making a move on the chessboard. No one speaks. The Finnish song "Levan Polka" plays in the background. On the table are a half-empty bottle of Olmeca and potato chips.

Grandma looks at the aquarium and says:

"No, no that was Comrade Chen, he was always a Kung Fu expert - ooh yes."

Tinfoil hat:

"How many of the cookies did she eat?"

Drag:

"I don't know, but I'd guess half the tray."

Tinfoil hat:

"And the body in the carpet?"

Drag:

"I guess the other half. Barf bag baked the cookies and went out to buy some junk food. By the time he got back, my grandma was here, and she and carpet corpse had already finished the whole tray, with a pot of Earl Gray tea."

The carpet unrolls. A bare-chested black man stands up, grabs his head with both hands and yells like Tarzan.

Grandma looks at the black guy:

"Oh; shi; I know that one, that's Jackie Chan."

Drag makes a move. No one pays any attention to the black man. Drag grabs a handful of chips.

Black:

"I think I have mini-minions in my brain, they are doing something with jackhammers. They're in my brain. They're building something, something important."

Tinfoil hat:

"The puke bucket has stopped puking."

Drag:

"No. He's passed out, but he keeps puking; look." Both look toward the man with the puke bucket, who, although fainted, still has a gag reflex.

"Grandma, will you make us something to eat?"

Black:

"I have to hurry" ... and starts jogging on the spot without moving on.

Chess game.

Drag:

"I'm hungry. Grandma ... will you make us something to eat?"

Tinfoil hat:

"Today of all days, your grandma had to come visit. And the carpet corpse thought your grandma baked the cookies."

Grandma:

"There are pigs coming out of that wall."

She goes to the aquarium and uses the fishing net to fish out the fish one by one and walks out of the room.

Black:

"I'm going to be late ..." and starts walking faster on the spot.

Chess game continues. Three minutes later, the grandma comes back into the room and serves Chinese instant noodles.

Tinfoil hat:

"Your grandma looks kind of green in the face."

Both look at the grandma. Then, Tinfoil hat:

"Hey Marathon Man ... you're out of danger ... come eat ..."

The black man stops walking and slowly comes to the table and joins the others.

Drag:

"Grandma, what is that you cooked? What is it?"

Grandma:

"These are Chinese yum-yum with pork."

Tinfoil hat:

"Gross! That's not pork. These are the fish from the aquarium."

Drag:

"Grandma, you killed my aquarium fish. You cooked my fish in the pasta."

Grandma:

"No, I haven't. The fish is raw, only the noodles are cooked."

Drag:

"Grandma, what's that? What did you cook?"

Grandma:

"I think it's Chinese sushi with yum-yum."

Tinfoil hat:

"Well, it's better than nothing."

Three people are at the table, but there are only two plates with food. The black man sits wordlessly at the table and does nothing. Grandma goes to the armchair, sits down and falls asleep.

Black:

"I'm tired, I'm going to sleep."

... and bangs his head on the table and starts snoring.

Tinfoil hat:

"Your aquarium fish with noodles tasted good. Your grandma is really a good cook. I'm tired too, I'm going to lie down in your bed."

Drag:

"Wait, I'll come with you. I need some sleep too. It's enough for today."

Tinfoil hat:

"Ok, but bring the nipple clamps ..."

"Well then, cheers," Dr. Neugebauer said and lifted his hand holding the bottle up in the air, "... to decadence ... and the umpteen deaths of Hans Moser, Theo Lingen, Loriot and Fernandel ..." He took a sip of Köstritzer, got up from the computer chair, went to the DVD player and put on an old movie. The Haunted Castle in Spessart, starring Liselotte Pulver. "Cool is whatever these fascist mutants think is uncool," he said as he turned on the TV and threw himself onto the leather couch. "I will have to schedule one night of old movies a week, just on principle ..."

"Homo Ludens, ego sum," he said aloud to himself. Culture is play; and play, according to the definition of the Brothers Grimm, is "an activity practiced not for the sake of a result or practical purpose, but for pastime, entertainment, and pleasure." Just to watch a movie without subliminal subconscious shock moments, just for feeling cheerful, he thought.

*

The next morning, Dr. Neugebauer was still under the decadent spell of this vulgarity and triviality, pondering the significance of this nipple-clamp sitcom story from the day before.

He launched into an attempt to analyze the subliminal message; the supposedly sarcastic sitcom garbage in combination with the description of conceptual arts ...

He remembered that he had come into contact with the concept of conceptual arts before. A "Russian" artist with the lovely name of Marius Shevanetkin, at a time when a Bulgarian was wrapping the Reichstag with paper, had the idea of rolling out toilet paper on a meadow while walking across it in an egg costume and having photos of this taken by a professional photographer. In extenuation of Russians, Dr. Neugebauer grinned inwardly, one should note that this "Russian artist" was most likely more of a Georgian melon seller than a Russian ... He had examined the photos at a vernissage about the freedom of the arts, while next to him a cleaning lady was scrubbing a bathtub smeared with mud. Thus, in a bizarre way, he became a witness to the perception of conceptual art by the simple man who defines himself through his work, the anthropological Homo Faber. It later turned out that this mud-smeared bathtub had been the main artwork of the vernissage, but the cleaning lady simply took the artwork for what it was, namely a filthy bathtub, which she cleaned without further ado. In the end, the pragmatic, commonsensical old cleaning lady, who, after learning that she had destroyed this work of art, suggested to get mud from the yard and make it filthy again, was not only fired but also sued for having destroyed a valuable work of art ...

Dr. Neugebauer looked out the window and thought ... He went to his desk, took out a blank sheet of paper, pondered for another moment and began to write briskly:

The semiotic analysis of conceptual art based on a sitcom sketch ...

He closed his eyes and recapitulated the principles of semiotics, a science that was not forbidden, but simply not taught anywhere ... The greatest and most important semiotician, he thought, was probably the Italian Umberto Eco. An out-and-out lateral thinker ... Through the centuries, lateral thinkers like Eco and Da Vinci had given continental Europe its greatness ... "Here's to lateral thinkers like Hermann Oberth and Max Planck, Mozart, Beethoven, and Ludwig Wittgenstein," he shouted, and, quoting Wittgenstein, raised a toast with his bottle of Köstritzer beer in the direction of an imaginary interlocutor: "The revolutionary will be the one who can revolutionize himself ..." He continued writing:

The narrative of the lateral thinker, formulated from the cultural anthropological approach to everyday life, has always postulated setting the absolutism of the traditional perspective and the perception of relative empirical reality by Homo Ludens, the playful human being, against holistic nonconformity ...

He closed his eyes again and recapitulated the axioms of semiotics: semiotics is not a methodological discipline, but a research field of various investigations. Dr. Neugebauer began to write again:

Culture: primary culture or multicultural? Primary culture of any kind is the basis of any civilization. Multiculti, on the other hand, exclusively produces independent tribal cultures, which also dilute this very culture until a cultureless monoculture remains. Europe's primary culture shaped the entire globe through occidental value creation and dynamic cultural dominance. Multiculturalism, on the other hand, is a system in which there is no longer an objective primary culture, but only subjective subcultures. Semiotics is the view of culture as a meta-linguistic sign system with its inherent communication variations. A symbol system that represents certain information qua agreement serves as a code. The existing rules and codes are results of cultural agreement and indoctrination, respectively. An important example is the paralanguage ...

He thought of his favorite words of the paralanguage: Robust mandate – means, the Bundeswehr will shoot people somewhere in the world ... Or the Dresden syndrome for women and children who make their fears known.

Likewise, the word fatherland, which, when uttered in isolation, creates an uneasy, stale, queasy feeling, which one is well advised to voice only in private. He wrote:

The Italian writer Ignazio Silone once said: When fascism returns, it will not say: "I am fascism". No, it will say: "I am anti-fascism". Through paralanguage, the authorities successfully initiated the reprogramming of German society. Friedrich Nietzsche paraphrases this nihilism and the decline of culture as the "valuelessness of the supreme values". Values, according to Nietzsche, are to be viewed in perspective through the respective "ruling structure" and are formed through the reevaluation of values. Not only National Socialist ideas were extracted by anthropological- educational applications; the entire canon of values of the Occident was not only questioned but likewise relativized, profaned and declared as fascism. Thus, Western European cultural man should feel guilty for the cultural creation of past centuries. Benito Mussolini described fascism in 1934 as follows: "Fascism should be called corporatism because it is the perfect fusion of the power of government and corporations." By the revolutionary conquest of the state and capitalist society as well as the collectivization of the peoples of Western Europe, a new stateless and classless social order is to be established in a system of anarcho-syndicalism. This system theory, coined in Europe, was symbiotically harmonized with the fascist ideal of corporatism. The newly installed system, however, goes a step further by imposing an anarcho-corporatism. Whereas National Socialism, on a degenerate völkisch-narcissistic level, still has at least a unique culture in the form of a monoculture comprising rudimentary cultural values, nihilistic anarcho-corporatism, as a cultureless form of social organization, represents the extreme political form of fascism, in which the individual, detached by absorption from any cultural qualities, has only a subjective subculture defined exclusively by consumption, in which the collective mass has value only as domesticated human capital. Since superordinate cultural values no longer exist (or are permitted to exist), collective identity is now atomized by the over-individualization of the population. The collective mass, which is culturally value-free in terms of content, the atomized subjects, define their value and habitus exclusively through consumption. The Marxian class struggle no longer exists in a nihilistic-value-absorbing system, since classes no longer exist apart from consumers separated into different segments. The monetary element, in principle an impersonal, arbitrary, imaginary primary actor, assumes the role of sovereign by virtue of its value-based properties. The individual framework of disposable money limits the intrinsic motivation of the individual and regulates the radius of his participation in society ... A conformist who dares to live, practice, or believe in common cultural, moral, or religious values transforms himself into a heretic within nihilistic anarcho-corporatism. The system then becomes the inquisition of the heretic. Thus, European cultural man assumes the role of the metaphorical "Jünger's animal", described by Ernst Jünger as "the situation of the domestic animal which entails that of the animal for slaughter ...". The dissolution of the capitalist system and the transition to anarcho-corporatism began when the state, now the new main actor in the socialist manner, decided which legal entity was declared relevant to the system and therefore required special protection. The conclusion, in

the words of Karlheinz Karius, is as follows:
The power of logic helps to answer questions.
The logic of power (on the other hand)
liquidates the questioner. Another semiotic
phrase is that of the "right-wing Nazi" as a
synonym for any nonconformist, the "wrong
thinker" who commits a "thought crime" in a
left-wing fascist system, in the system of
anarcho-corporatism, in which he raises a
question, such as, what else culture could be.
Immanuel Kant writes in this regard that
"...reason, however, is free by its nature and
does not accept orders to believe anything to be
true." In 1920, the National Socialists
generated the concept of "degenerate art",
which also included cultural trends. The
question raised as to what culture could be,
then leaves the authorities standing there
naked, as in Hans Christian Andersen's fairy
tale· The Emperor's New Clothes. By its
nature, fascism cannot even tolerate a
questioning in the subjunctive – let alone
allow a statement about the concept of the
status quo of the social order and the imposed
monoculture with impunity.

It is intolerable for the fascist if his
operational hierarchy of command is not
fully implemented, if the individual levels of
the hierarchy are not unconditionally

accepted or even questioned in their entirety. Thus, absolutist intolerance is the primary characteristic of the fascist. The more unqualified the system apparatchik, the political kapo, the faster his career opportunities within the fascist hierarchy chain. Because the only decisive criterion is unconditional obedience in line with the fascist agenda and total dependence on the fascist system. The system kapo is now just a lobbyist, a paid legionnaire in the orbit of the monetary authorities, which implicitly postulate precisely this in an educational context and present the prospect of advancement in the hierarchy and the transfer of potential mechanisms of power as a reward for absolute obedience. The perfidious thing now, however, is the perversion, undermining and reevaluation of the term Nazi. This turns the arsonist into the firefighter. Nazis are always the other nonconformists who can, may and should be hated with a clear conscience, since dissenters are not compatible with the fascist agenda and must at least be chastised as pariahs, at best even converted. But the petty-bourgeois narcissistic lackey, who forms the social foundation of the fascist system, will never realize that history is not only past static but also present dynamic, which induces conclusions regarding the future. Nonconformists, on the other hand, are always the culprits within the value system that reinterprets the semiotic keyword "fascist", regardless of whether they are Persians, South African blacks, Turkish literati or just average spiritual or pragmatic Germans who have something to share ... The Nazi cudgel is a directorial signal that the protagonist is required to integrate into the play, but before that, those whose brain synapses are not formatted according to the system agenda, should purify themselves through self-denial. Because the imperative hereditary guilt is accepted in the German subconscious, Nouveau Germans articulate themselves more objectively for Germany, because their perspective is a different one due to their schematic way of looking at things. The ontology of fascism creates the consistent dominance of the unical ideal as an obligatory fact within the thought pattern of the masses; the individual is only of relatively peripheral relevance here. The pathology of fascism is narcissistic self-aggrandizement through ego- inflation, which is stylized as a mass phenomenon. In contrast, there is the cultural man, Homo

Ludens, who lives and experiences patriotism as a healthy cultural habitus. Sense of home according to Carl Popper is a fundamental basis of pedagogy and a primary level on which the individual enters into social and cultural interaction with other individuals.

Sophie Scholl once said: "What we said and wrote, so many think."
She also said: "Stand by the things you believe in, even if you stand there alone."

Sophie Scholl's resistance to fascism grew out of her deep Christian faith and spirituality. By contrast, today you have the left fascist, the consumer-corporatist; and in his subconscious the paradigm is: "Consume! Because there is no God, no state, no fatherland, no flag, and no primary culture." In his authority status, the nihilistic consumer-corporatist declares cultural values as obsolete, because, within the concept of consumption and blind obedience to superiors, they are not seen as system-relevant or may even be regarded as hostile to the system. Nihilism in society is manifested in the collapse of the worldview and culture of Homo Ludens, man at play. This is anarchistic terror against culture, and abuse, rape and neutralization of aesthetics and thus the abolition of Homo Ludens Occidentalis, the playful man of the Occident, who defines cultural communication through the element of play. It is, so to speak, the absolute annihilation of the European man of culture. Ludwig Wittgenstein analyzed the materialistic culture based on the achievements of modern science and technology. His conclusion was that the kind of culture that leads humanity in the right direction is the spiritual culture based on eternal values. It is those eternal values that are at the core of the spiritual culture of humanity. The results of the industrial revolution, the irrational growth of markets, and the economics of greed evident in the imperialistic policies of governments are not, according to Wittgenstein, culture. Rather, culture for him included society's morality and decency, religion, ethics, language, and the way it conceives of the world and nature. Other semiotic codes are the musical facets, starting from the Pythagoreans who tried to describe a strictly structured system, to the discordant Death Metal as a music genre and a carrier of information and subconscious programming through shock effects and stress. Another axiom is the semiotics of architecture as an important principle ... How to analyze the symbolism of architecture with regard to programming the subconscious? What do the often-impersonal new buildings in Germany communicate to us architecturally? For example, why are all the buildings in Berlin low, usually only 4 stories high? What do skyscrapers symbolize? Only Frankfurt am Main, an inferior copy of the City of London, has skyscrapers. Architecture can be a signal of potency and a spirit of optimism, as in Alexanderplatz or Frankfurt am Main with the phallic symbolism of buildings rocketing skyward. It can also assert a claim to grandeur and power, like the buildings of Tempelhof Airport designed by Albert Speer. Or in the eastern part of the city, where neoclassicism prevails, in part alongside the Soviet claim to world dominance and uniformity. The semiotics of visual communication is the domain of corporatism ...

Dr. Neugebauer laughed sarcastically and thought: "They say that people have freedom; namely, the freedom to decide which TV program to watch, with which their subconscious will be reprogramed ... They didn't even bother to change the name ..."

We have the freedom to decide which TV program or YouTube channel will reprogram our subconscious or use it as a mental garbage dump ... And we, the news addicts who always have to be informed by what we think of as information, which is in fact an ongoing informercial, we miss the essence – namely, life itself. We pay with our lifetime for this paralyzing consumption of empty information overload. The human being is left behind as a driven person who no longer has time to stop and perceive the world as it is, without distortion. This is meant to say that the perspective of the left-fascist authorities is a distorted perception of the world and the associated canon of values, which contemptuously defines man as culturally value-free human capital and consumer.

The analysis of the sitcom was relatively simple ...

A black man, a transvestite, a Chinese woman, and a tinfoil hat.

The implementation of the politically correct. The white straight man and the white woman are meant to feel excluded from this. A large part of society is degraded to a minority. The drug of culture is used to spice it up, over-individualized and hedonistic. Life as consumption. We can perceive the result in all layers of society. Superhuman protagonists or marginal minority characters in each and every feature film ensure that visual communication in movie channels is raising generations for whom their own bodies are no longer sufficient and who feel within themselves an artificially generated need for a physical upgrade. The semiotic word for this is "beauty mania" ... An example is the tattoo fashion to refine one's own ego image, which in the past was only used by imaginary fringe groups. The tattoo in itself is a semiotic signal that the application of the revaluation of values is happening successfully. The realization of one's own physical inadequacy demands compensation in the form of increased consumption of luxury goods or culminates in extreme health mania.

Harald Neugebauer deliberated and continued writing:

The two main goals that were radically instigated by the Communist Party of Cambodia, called Angka, were:

1. Destruction of the country's intellectual elite and bourgeoisie to establish an impersonal precariat society. All

academically educated people were neutralized (a semiotic word for murdered), and higher education was abolished. Back to the Stone Age was the motto.

2. Destruction of the family and implementation of a pedagogy of values detached from traditional ties, with social norms that radically redefined the position of the individual in society.

All other events were the results of these paradigmatic upheavals. The education of children was carried out exclusively by the CP. The family in the classical value model was the enemy of the system and therefore obsolete. However, not only Cambodia serves as an application model for the left-wing fascists; there is also North Korea. When looking at North Korean transportation, you will notice that there are very few cars on the streets of Pyongyang. The population mainly uses buses, bicycles, or walks. The sociological idea behind this is not the Juche system's environmental protection of North Korea – it is much more simple: The mobility of the population is to be extremely restricted and strongly controlled.

But the perfidiousness of the EU left-wing fascists is that they go even further, thought Dr. Neugebauer.

Sexuality is no longer about "becoming one flesh", but instead, it is about hedonistic self-alienation and the illusion of freedom and individuality, of consumerism and high-performance sports. With early childhood sexualization through pornography as well as the hedonistic programing of pre-adolescent children, however, the zenith has not yet been reached. The gradual lowering of the voting age to 16 and eventually down to 14 gives the authorities the opportunity to satisfy the pedophile agenda through the backdoor of the right to vote, because whoever can vote also has the right to sexuality ...

The phone rang. The display read: Zoltan. "Hello Zoltan," Dr. Neugebauer said, "how ..." "She's dead," Zoltan's voice rasped in the receiver. "Henriette is dead." There was a long silence at both ends of the line. "What happened?" Dr. Neugebauer asked. "Henriette suddenly developed a thrombosis this morning and died." "What? How?" ... "Yes, she had a thrombosis," Zoltan cried with a yelp, "and she just passed away." "But ..." Dr. Neugebauer struggled to respond. Zoltan hung up. After about two minutes, the phone rang again. "Yes, Zoltan ... let's meet." "No," Zoltan replied. "You have the manuscript ... keep it safe ... There is a business card stapled to the last page ... call there ... Henriette was afraid of something like this." "Who's the business card from?" "It's the co-author's business card," Zoltan said. "After the funeral, I'm going to Prague with Alpaslan." "Who is Alpaslan?" Dr. Neugebauer asked. "The one who knows the co-author," Zoltan replied. "Don't come to the funeral, I'll meet you in Prague, later." And hung up again.

Editor: The reunion of the 3 protagonists in Prague, under whatever circumstances, is not of essential relevance to the story, it could be that this part impedes the flow and would detract from what the narrative intends.

Kimberly: All right, I'll keep it short then ...

Prague, May 1.

Dr. Neugebauer cried silently to himself and didn't care whether or not his tears flowed. He had not bathed in over a month and he smelled noticeably unpleasant. His matted and rudimentarily hand-combed hair was caked with dirt. Dr. Neugebauer knew he only had a few minutes before he would be discovered. He looked down at the bed where Zoltan lay. Zoltan's eyes, too, were glazed over and watery. Zoltan nodded almost imperceptibly with his eyes at Dr. Neugebauer, as if pleading for deliverance and absolution. "Yes, my good man, it will be all right," Dr. Harald Neugebauer whispered and faltered. His thyroid tensed ... He covered Zoltan Paskowiak's nostrils and mouth with his left hand and looked away from him. The latter began to twitch weakly and to tremble, emitting a rattling sound. The twitching lasted for more than two minutes. If Zoltan Paskowiak had been able to move, his will to survive would have reflexively snatched Dr. Neugebauer's hand away. But Zoltan could only quiver, paralyzed, in slow suffocation. Dr. Neugebauer, who had turned his head away, opened his tear-soaked eyes. His reddened gaze crossed that of the man lying in the neighboring bed. Alpaslan looked deep into his eyes. Dr. Neugebauer recognized in the pathetic creature's gaze a plea for help. But he couldn't, he couldn't. Zoltan's rattling had stopped. Zoltan was dead. Dr. Neugebauer had suffocated Zoltan. Panic erupted in his brain, a hurricane of emotion and mental pain. Alpaslan, who was lying in the next bed, tried to attract Dr. Neugebauer's attention with a slight, weak moan. Dr. Neugebauer did not have the strength to kill yet another human being. He looked helplessly and without hope into Alpaslan's eyes that sent out silent cries for salvation. But Harald Neugebauer could not. He ran out of the room without turning to look at Alpaslan again. Harald Neugebauer raced out and ran down the emergency stairs, exited the building and ran and ran until he could run no more, and his lungs burned like fire. He stopped abruptly, bent over, and screamed as loud as he could and began to cry loudly and uncontrollably.

*

Dr. Harald Neugebauer took a deep breath and entered the phone booth, which seemed to have been unused for a long time. He looked once again at the turquoise business card, which had a mobile phone number and the name Alpaslan written on the front. On the back of the business card was a Skype phone number with a U.S. area code. He read the words "Kurgan Börteçine." Dr. Neugebauer knew what these cryptic words meant. They came from the epic world of the Turkic peoples, not the Turks per se, but the mythical world of all those who saw or considered themselves in any way as Turks in the broadest sense.

A few years ago, on his study tour of China, he had visited the kurgans, the mound tombs of the Qing dynasty of Manchu rulers, in Xinbin

Autonomous Region, evidence of the last royal dynasty of the Yakut-Tungus people who, beginning with the ruler Nurhaci, ruled China for centuries. His journey also took him to the "Forbidden City" of the Chinese rulers, founded as Khanbalyk by the Uighur Turkic Mongol Genghis Khan in 1215. This was the self-image of the Turk, he thought bitterly ... The interwoven history of the Turk-Mongols told of the mother-wolf named "Börteçine," which was also the name of the blacksmith who forged the iron ore of the Turk and who broke through the iron mountain and unleashed the Turk on mankind. He took another deep breath, laughed bitterly and said: "Let Ali Baba, the barbarian, take back his man ..." The bell rang exactly three times ... ring-ring-ring. A man's voice at the other end of the line sounded: "Alo". Dr. Harald Neugebauer paused for a second, and the man on the other end of the line calmly repeated another "Alo." Dr. Neugebauer asked in a trembling voice: "German? English? Which language do you speak?" "Both languages," the man on the other end of the line replied in German. "It's about a man named Alpaslan who needs help," Dr. Neugebauer began. "I thought you might know him since his cell phone number is on this business card. Where did I just call, who am I speaking to?" After a brief pause, the man on the other end of the line asked dryly in a polite and calm voice: "What does it say below the phone number?" Dr. Neugebauer looked at the card and read. "It says Kurgan Börteçine." "One moment please, I'll put you through." There was a click, then another voice said: "Good afternoon." Dr. Neugebauer asked: "Who am I speaking to?" "Who am I speaking to?" asked the man on the other end of the line. "I, I'm..." - Dr. Neugebauer spoke quickly and briefly and in a decisive voice: "My name is Dr. Harald Neugebauer ..." "Pleased to make your acquaintance, Doctor," said the man on the other end of the line. Dr. Neugebauer said: "I know where Alpaslan is ... it's ... it's ... horrible ..." The unknown interlocutor took over in a calm tone and cryptically remarked: "Burgundy King. What is coming now is what God wanted to prevent." Dr. Neugebauer got goose bumps. "That's from the Nibelungenlied," he said in wonderment, softly and more to himself. "Where is he? And how many are there? " "There are many, very many, scattered over several countries," Dr. Neugebauer said. "He's in Prague." The man on the phone, quoting a poem by Bertold Brecht, said: "There are three emperors buried in Prague." "I'll give you the address," Dr. Neugebauer replied ... "Valiant Burgundian King, we owe you," the stranger said to Dr. Neugebauer. "Isn't it remarkable how history repeats itself?" "What do you mean?" Dr.

Neugebauer asked. "In the great aftershock following the First World War, old companions come together again, quite against their will. Just as the Ottomans and the Habsburgs and Prussians were allies in World War I, so our paths are crossing again for a higher purpose." "And against whom or what are we fighting?" Dr. Neugebauer wanted to know, suspiciously waiting for an answer. "Against the authorities of the global order, of course; anyone who has remained human can do nothing but that," the man on the line spoke with casual intonation. "We'll talk about the unofficial history later. Now let's make tabula rasa, Dr. Neugebauer, put aside your book Hannibal ante Portas. It's no longer about settling our trivial differences; it's about man himself, and nothing else ..." "What do you expect from us and from me?" Dr. Neugebauer asked. "Act as a mediator between us and your own ... We have some bastions in Europe, mainly in Hungary and Poland. You are already so far advanced epistemologically that you will realize that neither the Islam nor the Russian Ivan are your enemies, but those subjects. You fight for yourself, and we fight for ourselves, but all of us together against those subjects." "You're somewhat cryptic," Dr. Neugebauer said. The man on the other end began dictating an address. "Kiev bus station, across from the junk food restaurant you will find a snack bar with a kebab stand. Buy a kebab and an ayran there, then ask the vendor if he can make you some kefir. Everything else you will learn out there ..."

*

The Intercity Express sped toward Germany at breakneck speed. Dr. Harald Neugebauer couldn't help but think of Zoltan Paskowiak's book, in which Nietzsche ponders upon humanity while travelling on a train. He turned on his laptop and opened a news channel. Stunned, he stared at the computer screen. In the video, the old city of Prague was on fire. According to media reports, Pakistani, Arab, Afghan and black African paramilitary brigades were engaged in a private war against the Prague police. The heavy armament of the paramilitary gangs consisted of offensive weapons such as flamethrowers, hand grenades, firebombs, and even mortars and bazookas. Helpless, the Prague police had to call in the army for assistance and air support. Several helicopters had been shot down over the Old Town. By the time the unprepared Czech Army could rush to the rescue with old Sherman tanks left to the Europeans by the former NATO ally, the United States, as a parting gift after the disintegration of NATO in the second decade of the 21st century, Prague's historic Old Town was already consumed by flames. The well-organized brigades had come to the city in ordinary cars and motorcycles, all bearing EU license plates. Now Dr. Harald Neugebauer realized why the former NATO ally, the United States, had supplied its obsolete Sherman tanks to several European countries. These tanks, in use since the 1950s, were too antiquated for a modern war but ... but could be put to good use in a civil war. "Evil be to him who evil thinks," Dr. Neugebauer said. Among the dead paramilitaries were North Africans and black East and West Africans, Somalis and even Pakistani and Afghan so-called asylum seekers. The Russian-Turkish side would soon have to respond to the incidents ... A single word was written on the outer wall of Prague Castle in red letters about 3 meters high: - ITTIFAK - an Arabic word spelled out in Latin letters. Dr. Neugebauer knew this historical word only too well. It meant ALLIANCE. Could it be? Had the Islamic minorities joined together as an alliance in Europe? In order to ... yes, why actually?

Dr. Harald Neugebauer took a blank sheet of paper, thought briefly and wrote: The categorical imperative of Europe is the maxim of cultural dominance through value creation from culture in all areas and the conscious experience of tradition as well as historical awareness based on the last 2500 years of European cultural history.

"We Europeans are United in Diversity, but through the consciousness of our national cultures"... He smiled contemptuously ...

The anarchy, which the hegemonic authorities intensively and deliberately conjured up with the annihilation policy, the application of the Kalergi Plan in Europe, the "culturelessness as monoculture" and the destruction of the cultures of the Western European nation states by the politically left-wing fascist apparatchik kapos, has now been implemented ... Pol Pot ante portas, Dr. Harald Neugebauer further noted. The Schwarzkopf has suddenly become a temporary ally for a Europe that's rebelling against the Fuck-you-Goethe! simulation of society in Western Europe. We are the Christian Western Europe, wrote Dr. Neugebauer. The peoples of poets, of fine arts, of aesthetics, of thinkers and philosophers, of science, discipline, and order. The fascist, on the other hand, has always been against any kind of culture. For that reason, Hermann Goering quoted the German writer Hanns Johst: "When I hear the word culture, I take the safety catch off my Browning." By contrast, this is what Joschka Fischer said: "Nations make Europe, their culture, their language, their differences and their *similarities, and these nations are much older than nation states." But this quote belongs to an era long gone. Order always requires chaos to grow out of, and you, with your agenda, will fabricate anarchist chaos. We, however, we stand for human rights and order ... order out of chaos. If a savage dog corners a cat, at some point, before it is mauled, the cat will attack the dog and fight it with its two paws. We are beginning to organize, everywhere, regardless of how you report it or what you do ... Those who are spiritual you call esoteric .... People who dare to express their opinion you call Nazis. You disregard the Declaration of Human Rights, you bomb countries without a UN mandate, you give yourselves mendacious prizes. You have polarized and perverted democracy and society ...*

Dr. Harald Neugebauer had a dark premonition concerning the events now in their birth pangs, those dark clouds that were hovering over Europe ... "Imperium Magnum Infernalis," he said to himself. "Fuck you, too, Pol Pot, and all your kind!" he groaned. "This is the Occident ... And we are taking back our homeland from the fascists ..." He stood up, half-curled his arm in a clenched fist, and shouted across the rows of seats of the first-class carriage, quoting Friedrich Schiller:

"To the fatherland, to the dear one, join,

hold on to that with all your heart!

Here are the strong roots of your power."

A young man, part of a group of young people, murmured: "Fatherland??? Shut the fuck up, you uneducated redneck Nazi!" Shocked, they pointed their fingers at him, and one of them said: "You, you Nazi bastard! Get lost! Back to your Aryan pack in darkest East Germany, you miserable Nazi pig! I'll smack you right in your Nazi face, you fucking piece of shit, you brainwashed contrarian zombie!"

Another one set off to fetch the conductor. "Welcome to the game," Dr. Harald Neugebauer said, smiling at the mostly perplexed faces. He laughed out loud, looking at the reactions of the people in the first-class carriage. Most of them turned away and deliberately ignored the exchange of words between him and the young people. But a plain and unobtrusive couple sitting not far from him looked across without saying anything. The woman was carrying a baby in her arms. Dr. Neugebauer recognized the smile in the young couple's eyes and then spoke softly, nodding his head and looking deeply satisfied:

"Homo Ludens Occidentalis,
The European Cultured Man,
awaits you..."

EDITOR'S NOTES ON THE MANUSCRIPT:

My dear Kimberly!

It's nice that you want to put something on paper. BUT: What kind of borderline-crazy and provocative dystopia is this? Your manuscript is stuffed with pseudo-intellectual nonsense and housewifely analyses of our political system! You suffer from an obviously paranoid distortion of reality. Furthermore, you have used way too many quotes! Less is more. It reads as if you were in a delusional know-it-all fashion ... You are a smart-ass ... Anyone reading this book will immediately mistake you for one of the "Alt-Right" movement. You constantly subliminally praise Nazis such as the contrarians, the egalitarian movement, and anyone who falls off the edge of the table to the right in any way. And an Austrian at the end of your self-righteous story, standing with his arm raised, blathering on about fatherland, must be an incorrigible Nazi by his very nature. Of course, I recognized certain public figures and their arguments in your "epochal work". You are an oxymoron, a dinosaur living in the wrong time. <u>I am very disappointed in you as a person.</u> Neither young people nor the intellectual elite will be able to relate to this "work", this pamphlet, on principle because everything you write leaves an unpleasant aftertaste in those reading it. All these nebulous descriptions of the so-called elites and philanthropists that you hold responsible in your conspiracy theory, and all that you have written about our fellow Turkish and other Muslim citizens, is complete nonsense. Are you trying to stir up prejudice against Turks? And to drag our ecological agenda of environmental protection and climate change through the mud like this and compare it to Angka and Juche communism, that is malicious. Germany is a welfare state that respects and protects the rights of everyone, yes EVERYONE. You know that our social consensus is built on solidarity, namely solidarity with the weakest in society. We are pioneers in the European Union in all that we do. Don't you know how many of your so-called "Turks trapped in social apathy" have made careers for themselves in free enterprise, politics, and the natural sciences? If you want to publish this pamphlet about fascism, you should think about revising your work and rewriting it to conform to reality. Or else self-publish it. If you want to change society, vote in the elections, and get involved with a political party. Because that's the way democracy works. I am saddened to see that there are people in Germany who still sympathize with fascist ideology. Germany is a constitutional state, and fascism will not be tolerated in this country. I hereby resign my position as editor.

Respectfully,

Editor.

The editor closed the manuscript, opened his journal, and wrote:

I hope that these formulations are politically compliant in the new Germany. Once upon a time, this was our homeland. Many of my friends have served in the Bundeswehr, many have defended Germany in disputes in foreign countries against people from other cultures, whether in Asia or elsewhere. But today we are like strangers within German society. You have alienated us to such an extent that this is no longer our homeland. You have robbed me of my homeland. It's time to pack our bags. Let them, the right-wing left-wingers and the left-wing right-wingers, who between them have garbaged up society and their brains to the point where the synapses are completely gummed up, deal with it themselves. None of this concerns me anymore. I carry my Germany in my heart, in the memories of my youth, when there was a "we".

How on earth could you lose three million people to such alienation and kanak precarization from mainstream society?

That night on November 9, 1989, around 3:00 a.m., I was listening to "Rias 2," the radio station in the American sector of Berlin, and studying for my next-day English exam, when the presenter suddenly made the announcement that a crowd was beginning to gather at Checkpoint Charlie on the east side. That night, the Wall fell. The next day, my English exam was postponed, which I would not have passed anyway. My mother, my sister and I sat in front of the television and watched, spellbound, the historical events that were unfolding in Berlin. Back then, my mother, crying because of the pictures, said: "It is not right to separate a people in such a way. Finally, this injustice is over." The past and the present are lost forever, only the future is valid now. My bags are packed, in my mind's eye I am already waiting in the *departure hall of the new Berlin-Brandenburg airport, the symbol of a new, different Germany. I will not forgive you all for making me a homeless person.*

Derya Yalimcan, 09.11.2021

The editor put the fountain pen on the desk, which was in the kitchen next to the balcony. He took the bottle of Köstritzer beer from the table and in his imagination clinked bottles with the black and white portrait hanging on the kitchen wall to his left. It showed the image of a man in military uniform with a neat mustache and an old-fashioned, rimless high Turkish uniform cap made of Astrakhan wool. The man in the effigy looked at the editor with deep, serious, and bright eyes. The editor returned the gaze and said, quoting the man in the effigy:

"Civilization is like a blazing flame that consumes anyone who thinks they can ignore this."

- END -

A novella by Derya Yalimcan under the pseudonym Harald Neugebauer